SOPHIE IS SEVEN

"In the fifth story from this master storyteller about Sophie ... she is even more incredible than before in her ideas, her witty replies, and her determination... Children will, of course, love it." *The Junior Bookshelf*

Dick King-Smith used to be a farmer and is now one of the world's favourite children's book authors. Winner of the Guardian Fiction Award for *The Sheep-Pig* (filmed as *Babe*), he was named Children's Book Author of the Year in 1991 and won the 1995 Children's Book Award for *Harriet's Hare*. His titles for Walker include the Read and Wonder non-fiction picture books *All Pigs Are Beautiful* and *I Love Guinea-Pigs*, as well as *Puppy Love*, *Dick King-Smith's Animal Friends* and *The Finger Eater*.

David Parkins has illustrated a number of children's books, including the picture books *No Problem*, *Prowlpuss* (shortlisted for the 1994 Kurt Maschler Award and the Smarties Book Prize), *Aunt Nancy and Old Man Trouble* and *Aunt Nancy and Cousin Lazybones*.

"Bit dirty," said Sophie cheerfully. *"And a bit pongy."*

SOPHIE
IS SEVEN

Written by
DICK KING-SMITH

Illustrated by
DAVID PARKINS

WALKER BOOKS
AND SUBSIDIARIES
LONDON • BOSTON • SYDNEY

"I could walk ten miles," Sophie said.
"Couldn't I, Tomboy?"

Sophie in the Garden

One day in late autumn Sophie sat on the edge of her bed, holding her piggy-bank. She had just stuck a fresh label on its side. The first label, when she was only four, had said:

Farm munny
thank you
Sophie

Later, she had crossed out MUNNY and written MONNEY instead, and now, getting on for seven, she had designed a new label that read:

Farm Money. Please Give Genrusly.
Thank You. Sophie

Sophie unscrewed the plug in the pig's stomach and tipped out the contents and counted them. They came to twelve pounds, sixty pence.

She looked round the walls of her bedroom at the pictures, drawn by her mother, of a cow called Blossom, two hens called April and May, a spotty pig named Measles and a pony named Shorty.

These were the animals she would buy once she became a lady farmer. Sophie, though very small, was very determined, and no one in the family doubted that she would one day achieve her ambition.

Now she rubbed the tip of her nose, a sign that she was thinking deeply.

"Twelve pounds, sixty," said Sophie, "is

not enough. I shall have to raise some more money, somehow."

At that moment her twin brothers Matthew and Mark burst into the room. Matthew was ten minutes older than Mark, and both were two and a bit years older than Sophie, and neither of them ever walked when he could run or spoke quietly when he could shout.

"Wow!" they cried with one voice, at the sight of the money spread upon Sophie's bed. "How much have you got?"

"Twelve pounds, sixty," said Sophie, "and where are your manners?"

"What d'you mean?" they said.

"You should knock before you come into a lady's bedroom. You're rude, you are."

"And mowldy," said Matthew.

"And stupid," said Mark.

"And assive," they both said, for this was

how an angry Sophie had always described them.

They grinned at one another.

"I know!" said Mark.

"I know what you're going to say!" said Matthew.

"And so do I," said Sophie, "and the answer is NO. I am not going to lend you any money, not one penny."

"Meanie!" they cried, and off they dashed, racing one another down the stairs.

Sophie put all the money back in the piggy-bank and screwed up its stomach again. Then she plodded downstairs and stood it on the hall table, where anyone who came to the house would, she hoped, read its message. Then she went to find her mother.

"Mum," she said. "How do you raise money?"

"For a good cause, d'you mean?" her mother said.

"Yes. A very good one."

"Like Children in Need, that sort of thing?"

"Yes," said Sophie.

I am a child in need, she thought.

"Well, there are all sorts of ways. You can have jumble sales, or raffles, or things like sponsored walks."

"What's that mean?" asked Sophie.

"Well, people set out to walk a certain distance – ten miles, let's say – and other people agree to pay a sum of money for each mile they manage to go. Ten pence a mile, perhaps."

"Or one pound a mile?" said Sophie.

"Possibly."

"That'd be ten pounds."

"Yes, and if you persuaded ten people to

11

sponsor you at one pound a mile, and then you walked ten miles, that'd be a hundred pounds for the good cause."

"Yikes!" said Sophie softly.

Ten miles, she thought. I bet I could walk ten miles. It's not like a marathon, you don't have to run.

Later she said to the twins, "How far is a marathon?"

"Twenty-six miles," said Matthew.

"And three hundred and eighty-five yards," said Mark.

Sophie went off to the potting-shed where once she had kept her flocks and herds of snails and slugs and centipedes and suchlike creatures. Now only her white rabbit Beano lived there in his large hutch.

Sophie discussed the matter with him.

"Just walking ten miles is easier than running more than twenty-six, wouldn't you say, my dear?" she asked him. "Miles easier."

Beano, a large rabbit with floppy ears, stared at her with his red eyes. He had a wiffly nose, and now he wiffled it at Sophie, in agreement, she thought.

Then Sophie's black cat Tomboy poked her nose around the door of the shed.

"I could walk ten miles," Sophie said. "Couldn't I, Tomboy?"

"Nee-o," said the cat, or that was what it sounded like. Sophie looked out at the garden. It was a rough square in shape, and there was a gravelled path that ran right round it. Sophie plodded right round it, once.

"I wonder how far that was," she said.

That evening she asked her father, "Daddy, how far is it round our garden?"

"Round the path, d'you mean?"

"Yes. Half a mile, d'you think?"

Sophie's father laughed.

"I'll pace it out for you if you like," he said. "My step is about a yard long. Why d'you want to know, anyway?"

"I just do," Sophie said.

So her father walked solemnly round all four sides of the garden, counting aloud.

"Eighty-nine," he said at the end. "Call it eighty-eight, it makes it easier, because then ten times round would be eight hundred and eighty yards, or half a mile."

"Yikes!" said Sophie. "So if you wanted to walk a mile, you'd have to go round..." She paused for thought.

"Twenty times!" her father said.

"What if someone wanted to walk ten miles?"

"Two hundred times. If anyone was mad enough to do it. Satisfied now? Because I want to go in and watch the cricket on TV."

14

Two hundred times, Sophie thought. Still, I bet I could do that.

In the sitting-room she found Matthew and Mark, who were keen on all sport, also watching the cricket. Puddle, the family's dog, a small white terrier with a black patch over his right eye, sat in front of the television set, quivering with eagerness. One thing he loved was chasing a ball, and he could see one there, being bowled or thrown or hit. Just let it come out of that box and he'd have it! Sophie stared at the screen absently, her mind full of this scheme – so simple, it seemed – for raising money.

Suppose Daddy gave a pound for each mile, and Mum another one, and the twins – no, more likely they'd give a penny. She'd have to get a lot of other people to pay, so as to raise a lot more Farm Money. Like everyone at school perhaps. Except

Dawn, of course. Dawn was a girl with whom Sophie had often tangled in the past and she would certainly not give anything at all.

Still, the first thing to be done was to walk the ten miles. Then she could tell everybody she'd done it and then they'd pay up. First thing tomorrow, said Sophie to herself, I'll do it. Now, that decided, she paid some attention to the cricket. After a bit she said, "It looks nice and sunny where they're playing, so why is that man wearing a hat and a white coat and a sweater round his neck and another sweater tied round his middle? Is he cold?"

"No," they all said. "He's one of the umpires."

"The bowlers take off their sweaters to bowl," said Mark.

"And he looks after them," said Matthew.

16

"What a nice man," said Sophie.

A little later she said, "Why's he doing that?"

"Who?" said Matthew.

"The empire."

"Umpire," said Mark. "Doing what?"

"Taking something out of one of his pockets and putting it in the other one."

"Those are pebbles," said her father. "He's counting how many balls the bowler's bowled. When he's transferred six pebbles from one pocket to the other, he says 'Over'."

"Why?" said Sophie.

"It's the end of the over. Then everyone changes ends. They all cross over."

"Over what?" said Sophie.

"Oh, do be quiet, Sophie," said the twins.

"Just watch for a bit, Sophie," said her father, "and you may get the hang of it."

17

"No, I won't," said Sophie, and she stumped off, scowling.

By the time Sophie went to bed that night her plans were laid. First thing tomorrow she would do that ten-mile walk. Going round the garden two hundred times was sure to take quite a while, so, she thought, I must make an early start. She banged her head on the pillow six times, and went straight to sleep.

When she woke, she looked at her watch and saw to her surprise that it was indeed exactly six o'clock.

Sophie dressed quickly, crept downstairs, put on her wellies, and went out, Puddle at her heels, into a damp, overcast morning.

"We'll start by the potting-shed, my dear," she said to Puddle, "and when we come round to it for the two hundredth time, that'll be it. Simple. Except we'll have to keep count or we might go round too many times."

"Got it!" she said, and she bent and picked up a handful of bits of gravel from the path and put them in the pocket of her jeans. Then she opened the potting-shed door, said "Good morning" to Beano, gave him a carrot, and found an old cardboard box which had BAKED BEANS in black print on one side and on the other SNALES in big red capitals.

She put the box down in the doorway and set off around the garden path, Puddle following. As she passed the potting-shed after the first circuit, she took a piece of gravel from her pocket and dropped it into the cardboard box.

"Only a hundred and ninety-nine to go!" said Sophie to Beano, and plodded on. From the leaden sky a few large drops began to fall.

At half past six Sophie's mother was woken by the rattle of raindrops against her window-pane.

She got out of bed without disturbing her sleeping husband and went to look out into the garden. It needs rain, she thought. There below her was Sophie, plodding solemnly around the garden path in the steady downpour.

As her mother watched in amazement, she reached the open door of the potting-shed, took something from her pocket, threw it into a box, and stumped on, Puddle trotting after.

Sophie's mother hurried downstairs, threw a macintosh over her nightclothes and ran for the potting-shed through the teeming rain. Hardly had she reached its shelter than Sophie appeared again outside its door, a piece of gravel in her hand.

Hardly had Sophie's mother reached the shelter of the potting-shed than Sophie appeared.

"Sophie!" her mother cried. "Come inside here straight away!"

Sophie came into the shed. Her dark hair, which always looked as though she had just come through a hedge backwards, now looked as if she had just swum the Channel. It was plastered to her head, and her clothes – old jeans and an old much-too-small blue jersey with her name written on it in white letters – were sopping wet. Her wellies squelched. Puddle, who loved water, came in too and shook himself happily over them.

"What in the world have you been doing?" Sophie's mother said.

"Walking," said Sophie shortly.

"In all this rain? Round and round the garden path? Why?"

"To raise money. For a good cause. Like you said."

"A sponsored walk, you mean?"

Sophie nodded, dripping.

"What were you trying to raise money for?"

"My farm," said Sophie. "I've only got twelve pounds, sixty."

Her mother looked fondly at her small but determined daughter.

"Come into the house," she said, "and we'll get those wet things off and put you in a nice hot bath."

"But I haven't finished my walk," Sophie said.

"Yes, you have. Come on."

"Oh, all right then," Sophie said. "Just wait half a minute," and she began to count the pieces of gravel in the SNALES box.

"Twenty," she said.

"You mean you've been round twenty times?"

"Yes. That's a mile, Dad said. I've still got nine miles to do."

In the bath Sophie sat playing with a rubber frog that squeaked. Puddle, rubbed dry now, sat on the mat hopefully. Just let it hop out of that bath and he'd have it!

"So how much money d'you think I'll get for walking a mile?" Sophie said.

"Sophie love," said her mother gently. "You've got things a bit muddled. A sponsored walk means that you have to go round to everyone *before* you do the walk and get them to sponsor you. *Then* you do the walk, and then they pay up."

"Oh," said Sophie.

"And usually people walk a long way across country, not just round and round the garden."

"Oh," said Sophie. "So I shan't get

anything?"

"Well," said her mother, "let's pretend that I did sponsor you. How far did you say you'd gone?"

"A mile."

"Then I'll give you one pound."

Sophie grinned.

"Thanks, Mum," she said. "Actually I was quite glad to stop. I did want to do ten miles but I don't think I'd have had the stanima."

"Stamina, you mean."

"Yes. Can we have breakfast now? I'm starved."

"Some people are ingerant," said Sophie,
and she pointed her pencil at Dawn.

Sophie in the Classroom

Sophie enjoyed school. She quite liked the teachers – they were all right – and she did not mind the other children (except Dawn), though she did not make friends easily.

Partly this was because she was perfectly happy on her own, and partly it was because a good number of the other children were, in her opinion, either wimps (like Dawn) or wallies (like Duncan, a very small boy with ginger hair, short legs and a fat stomach). At one point Sophie had considered taking on Duncan as a farm labourer when she should become a lady farmer, but later she had sacked him.

She did, however, approve of one boy, Andrew, a farmer's son, and she sometimes contrived to go to tea at the farm (by telling Andrew to ask his mother to ask her). Like Jo, a girl she had met on a recent Cornish seaside holiday, Andrew smelled nice to Sophie. Jo smelled of pig and horse, Andrew of cow.

The only thing about school to which Sophie objected was that they didn't have Farming Lessons.

"I can't understand why they don't," she said. "It's all very well to teach me to read and add up and stuff like that, but how am I going to become a lady farmer if they don't teach me farming?"

"You have to be taught lots of other things first," said her father.

"And you've got plenty of books about farms," her mother said. "You could learn quite a bit from them."

"Or from Andrew," said Mark.

"Your boyfriend," said Matthew.

"He's not my boyfriend," said Sophie angrily. "He's my friend."

"Well, if he's your friend..." said Matthew.

"...and he's a boy," said Mark.

"...then he's your boyfriend," they said.

"You," said Sophie, "are mowldy, stupid and assive!" and she stumped off.

But after half-term Sophie had a pleasant surprise.

On the first day back at school, her teacher said to the class, "Now then, children, the topic we are all going to do for the next few weeks is Farming."

"Yikes!" cried Sophie.

"I thought you would be pleased, Sophie," said the teacher, "and I expect you will be too, Andrew."

Andrew, a sturdy little boy of about Sophie's height and build, but with very fair, almost white, hair, said loftily, "I know all about farming already."

"How clever," said the teacher. "Then you'd better keep quiet for a minute while I ask the rest of the class some questions. Now then, where does milk come from?"

A forest of hands shot up.

"Well, Dawn?"

"Out of a bottle," said Dawn.

Sophie gave a snort.

Dawn looked to her even more revolting than usual. As well as the green bows with which her bunches of fair hair were always tied, she wore little gold earrings and her fingernails were painted coral pink.

"Well, Sophie," said the teacher, "is Dawn right?"

"She's ingerant," Sophie said.

"You mean ignorant."

"I mean soft in the head," said Sophie. "Milk comes out of a cow."

"She's right, you know," said Andrew.

"Yes, I daresay she is, but there's no need to be so rude to Dawn, Sophie. And anyway, since you know all about it, tell us why the cow has milk."

"To feed its baby of course," said Sophie. "All mothers do. I shall one day, after I'm married."

"Yes, yes," said the teacher. "Let's just stick to cows for the moment. Now then, someone – not Sophie or Andrew – tell me, what is a cow's baby called?"

"A calf!" said several voices.

"You have to have a bull," said Sophie.

"She's right, you know," said Andrew.

"Yes, yes, quite right, Sophie," said the

teacher hurriedly. "Now then, what other animals do farmers keep?"

The forest of hands sprouted again.

"Sheep," said someone.

"Pigs," said someone else.

"Horses," said Duncan, who had spent some time as a horse in the playground, being lunged on the end of a skipping-rope. At first he had been Sophie's horse, but later, when Sophie was away with chicken-pox, he had trotted around Dawn. On Sophie's return that had all ended in tears (not Sophie's).

"Farmers don't have horses," said Andrew scornfully. "They have tractors. We've got a big green one. Cost half a million pounds, it did."

"I'm sure there are still a few farmers that use horses," the teacher said. "But you've all forgotten about some other creatures. What about birds? What sort of birds would a farmer keep?"

"Chickens," said someone.

"And ducks and geese," said someone else.

"Ostriches," said Sophie.

There were giggles and sniggers, especially from Dawn.

"Don't be silly, Sophie," said the teacher.

Sophie's face darkened.

"They do," she said. "They do have ostrich farms, I saw it on the telly."

"She's right, you know," said Andrew.

"Just be quiet, both of you," said the teacher. "Now we've mentioned chickens and ducks and geese, but we've forgotten another sort of bird. A big one, it is."

"Ostriches are big," said Sophie.

"No, no, this is a bird that we connect with a very special day, not many weeks away now."

Everyone looked blank, so the teacher said, "The twenty-fifth of December. What's that?"

"My seventh birthday," said Sophie.

"Yes, yes, but what else?"

"Christmas Day!" said Dawn.

"Yes, so what bird am I talking about?"

"A turkey!"

"That's right. Everyone looks forward to Christmas dinner, don't they?"

"No," said Sophie. "The turkeys don't."

"I'm beginning to think," said Sophie's teacher to the others as she drank her coffee in the staff room at break, "that I shouldn't have chosen Farming as a topic. I'm not quite sure who's teaching the class, me or Sophie and Andrew."

Later she set the children to draw and colour

pictures, to make a display for the classroom walls.

"Choose something to do with farming," she said.

Most of them set to work to draw an animal of some kind, though Andrew began a picture of a very large tractor with a very small figure (himself) driving it, and began to colour it green.

The teacher approached Sophie's place somewhat nervously. I bet she's drawing an ostrich, she thought. Or a turkey, probably being chased by a man with an axe.

But in fact Sophie had drawn a very fat cow.

Beneath the exact centre of its huge belly was an enormous udder.

"Goodness!" said the teacher. "She must be a good milker."

"She is," said Sophie shortly.

The teacher pointed at the four large, stiff sausage shapes sticking out beneath the udder.

"Those are a bit big, aren't they?" she said.

"What, her tits?" said Sophie.

"Teats, they're called."

"Farmers call them tits," said Sophie.

"She's right, you know," said Andrew.

"That's where the milk comes out, you see," said Sophie.

"Yes, Sophie, I think we all know that."

"You can't be sure," said Sophie. "Some people are ingerant," and she pointed her pencil at Dawn.

Hastily the teacher said, "What are you going to call your cow, Sophie?"

"Blossom," said Sophie.

"That's a nice name. Though I still think you've drawn her rather too fat."

36

"Of course she is," said Sophie. "That's because she's just going to have a calf. I told you, didn't I? About the bull. Remember? Then nine months afterwards the cow gets very fat and very full of milk, see?"

"She's right, you know," said Andrew.

The cat made straight for Sophie and wound itself around her legs, purring like a steam-engine.

SOPHIE AT THE STABLES

"Mum?" said Sophie one Saturday morning.

"Yes?"

"When can I start having riding lessons?"

"Not till after Christmas. You remember Aunt Al's offer."

Sophie remembered all right. She had done some riding when they were on holiday in Cornwall, and had loved it, and had told Aunt Al all about it.

Aunt Al was really Sophie's great-great-aunt, but they were also great, great friends. Though one was not yet seven and the other had just passed eighty-two, they were very much the same sort of person. Each was small and determined, and each took a no-nonsense approach to life's problems.

At the end of the holidays Aunt Al had offered to pay for Sophie to have riding lessons locally, as a combined Christmas and birthday present.

"It's a long time to wait," Sophie said now to her mother.

"Only a matter of weeks."

"But where shall I have the lessons?"

"At a riding school."

"But I don't know any."

"I expect there are lots round about. Look in the *Yellow Pages*."

Sophie plodded off and found the *Yellow Pages* directory and opened it in the middle of the Rs.

"Removals – Rest Homes – Restaurants – ah, here we are, Riding Schools," she said to

Tomboy, who was snoozing on the sofa. She stroked her black back.

"I am going to learn to ride really properly, my dear," she said, "like a lady farmer should. Let's see if we can find one that's nice and near."

There were quite a number within easy distance of Sophie's home, but one particular advertisement caught her eye.

CLOVERLEA STABLES
• Children and beginners welcome
• Learn to ride and enjoy the freedom of the countryside
• Day, half-day or hourly
• Ponies for sale

Sophie looked at that last line. Just imagine, she thought.

"You never know," she said to Tomboy. "Once upon a time I didn't have an animal of my own. Then I got you, my dear, and then my own rabbit, and then my own dog," (for Sophie preferred to think of Puddle as hers, rather than the family's) "so how about my own pony?"

"Neee-o," said Tomboy.

"It might just fit in the potting-shed if it wasn't too fat, and riding round the garden two hundred times would be much easier than walking."

Sophie rubbed the tip of her nose. The twins had gone out with their father, she knew, and, looking out of the window, she saw that her mother was pruning her rose bushes. Sophie dialled the number of Cloverlea Stables.

"Have you a pony for sale, suitable for a child of nearly seven?" she said.

"You want to buy a pony?" said a woman's voice at the other end.

"Yes."

"As a matter of fact I have. Is it for a beginner?"

"Sort of," said Sophie.

"I've a very pretty little child's pony, a palomino mare, twelve hands, quiet as a lamb."

And not too fat, I hope, thought Sophie.

"How much?" she said.

"I couldn't take less than a thousand pounds."

"Oh," said Sophie. "I've only got thirteen pounds, sixty."

"Oh dear," said the woman. "That wouldn't even cover two riding lessons."

"Yikes!" said Sophie. "How much are they then?"

"Eight pounds an hour. That's with a small group of other children."

Sophie was silent. Aunt Al once gave me

five pounds for my birthday, she thought, so I suppose she just might make it eight pounds this time. But that's only for an hour. How am I going to learn to ride really well in an hour?

"Are you still there?" asked the voice at the other end.

"Yes."

"Well, why not get your mummy or daddy to give me a ring? Then we can talk about it."

"OK," said Sophie. "You'd better not say anything about me wanting to buy a pony, if you don't mind."

"I won't say a word," said the woman.

"Thanks," said Sophie. "See you soon."

I hope, she thought as she put the phone down.

She went out to her mother.

"I phoned up a riding school," she said.

"Did you? Good. When you do start we must see if they'll sell us a bag of horse manure. It'd do these roses a power of good."

Buy me a pony, thought Sophie, and you can have as much manure as you like, free.

"The lessons are very expensive," she said.

"How much?"

"Eight pounds an hour."

"I'm not surprised."

"Aunt Al will be," said Sophie.

"Perhaps you'd better telephone her," said her mother.

So Sophie did.

Aunt Al lived in the Highlands of Scotland, right on the very tip-top of them, Sophie always imagined, surrounded by golden eagles and blue hares and red deer.

Sophie had spoken to her on the phone

several times before, and it always amazed her to think of her voice rushing along all those hundreds of miles of telephone wires and then finally right up the steep slopes of those very high Highlands, and then of Aunt Al's voice rushing all the way back down again. And all just as quick as if she was in the room, and as clear too.

"Hullo, Aunt Al," she said. "It's me."

"Sophie!" said Aunt Al. "How nice to hear your voice. How's everyone?"

"Oh, Tomboy and Beano and Puddle are fine," said Sophie.

"I meant your parents really, and the boys."

"Oh, they're OK. How's Ollie?"

Ollie was Aunt Al's cat, a son of Tomboy.

"He's just fine. I'm fine too."

There was a pause while Sophie tried to decide how to break the news. She'll have a fit when she hears how much, she thought.

"Was there something special you were ringing up for?" said Aunt Al.

"Yes," said Sophie. She did not approve of beating about the bush, so now she came straight out with it.

"Those riding lessons you said you'd give me."

"Well?"

"They're ever so expensive."

"How much?"

"Eight pounds an hour."

All the way down that long line from the Highlands came a long, low whistle.

"Are they indeed?" said Aunt Al.

"Yes," said Sophie. "So I'm just ringing up to say thank you very much but I don't think I could learn to ride really well in an hour so perhaps we'd better forget it."

"Load of rubbish!" said Aunt Al. "Now

you listen to me, Sophie. If I remember rightly, I offered to pay for a course of riding lessons, as a combined Christmas and seventh birthday present. Didn't I?"

"Yes."

"Well, then a course of riding lessons is what you're going to have. Get it?"

"Yes."

"If you're going to learn to ride, then you're going to learn to ride properly, understand?"

"Yes."

"I did, when I was your age, and I've never regretted it. Just don't get any crack-brained ideas about having a pony of your own. It'd cost the earth to buy, let alone keep."

"Yes. Thanks, Aunt Al."

"Goodbye then."

"Goodbye."

★　★　★

So the next day Sophie went to Cloverlea Stables.

Her father was playing golf, and Matthew and Mark were playing football as usual, so Sophie's mother said to her, "Let's go and have a look at this riding school you phoned up. We want to make sure that Aunt Al's money is going to be well spent," and she rang up and fixed a time.

In the stable yard they got out of the car to see a number of faces looking out at them over the half-doors of a row of loose-boxes. Then round the corner of the block came a large, tall lady, closely followed by a tortoiseshell-and-white cat.

Something about them both was familiar to Sophie.

The cat made straight for her and wound itself around her legs, tail stiffly upright, purring like a steam-engine.

*In the stable yard they got out of the door to see a
number of faces looking out at them.*

"Well," said the large, tall lady, "Dolly seems to like you."

"Sophie's good with animals," her mother said.

"Sophie?" said the large, tall lady, and she looked hard at her.

"Dolly?" said Sophie, and she looked hard at the cat.

"Got it!" said the large, tall lady. "You're the little girl I bought Dolly from as a kitten. I remember now, you just had the one queen. The others were all toms, and I seem to recall you were a bit miffed about that."

"I was," said Sophie. "I hoped they were all female and then I could have bred loads of kittens and sold them to make money for my farm."

"So you're going to be a farmer?"

"A lady farmer."

"Quite so," said the riding school owner, whose name was Meg Morris. "In that case, learning to ride would be a good idea so that one day you can ride round your farm. Have you ever been on a pony before?"

"Yes," said Sophie. "Last summer. In Cornwall. He was called Bumblebee. I fell off once."

"But she got straight on again," said Sophie's mother, "and before the end of the holiday she actually hopped over some little jumps."

"Good," said Meg Morris. "Then I needn't treat her as an absolute beginner. When would you like her to start?"

"Today," said Sophie.

"After Christmas," said her mother.

"I couldn't fit you in yet anyway, Sophie," said the large, tall lady. "I'm pretty booked up. Let's have a look in the diary."

Inside an old stable that served as an office, Meg Morris said, "Now then, Christmas Day is on a Saturday this year, so the following Saturday will be New Year's Day, and it just so happens that I'm starting a new group then. Five is the maximum number I teach at one time, and I've already got four little girls booked, so Sophie would make five. How about that? Saturday, January the first, ten o'clock?"

"Fine," said Sophie's mother. "And now we must be off."

"Goodbye, Dolly, I must leave you," said Sophie, giving the tortoiseshell cat a final stroke.

"She's a wonderful mouser," said Meg Morris. "I can't remember what I paid you for her but she's been worth every penny of it."

"Five pounds," said Sophie, "and that

reminds me."

She fished in her pocket and brought out the one pound coin that her mother had given her for the sponsored walk.

"Do you sell horse dung?" she said.

"Yes. There's some bagged up, at the other end of the yard."

"I want a bagful, please, for Mum's roses," said Sophie. "How much?"

"To you, Sophie," said the large, tall Meg Morris, "nothing. Take it as a present from Dolly and me."

"Thanks," said Sophie. "I'm very gracious." And she plodded off down the yard.

"She means 'grateful'," said her mother.

"She means well," said Meg Morris.

In the car on the way home Sophie's mother said, "That was very nice of you to think of buying me that manure."

"That's all right, Mum," Sophie said.

She twisted round to look at the bulging bag on the back seat.

"Yikes!" she said happily. "What a lovely pong! It's delirious!"

Sophie flapped her elbows, stretched out her short neck and hissed back at the gander.

SOPHIE ON THE COACH

No one entering Sophie's classroom could be in any doubt about what topic the children were doing.

The walls were covered with drawings and paintings of all things agricultural. As well as Sophie's hideous cow and Andrew's enormous tractor, there were flocks and herds of every animal you could possibly expect to see on an English farm. There were also several that you would have been surprised to come across (zebras, for example, and a solitary polar bear).

There were pictures of cowsheds and cornfields, of haystacks and henhouses, of duckponds and Dutch barns, and a great many pieces of descriptive writing about life on the farm.

There were also several poems, one of which was by Sophie.

Underneath a picture of a heap of tin cans and bottles, and car tyres, and an old TV set with a busted screen, she had written:

Do not be a litter lout
And throw your rubbish about
Always put your bottle or tin
In a rubbish bin
Another thing farmers hate
Is if you don't shut the gate
Because his animals will stray
And some will run away
And keep your dog on a lead
Or it may chase the sheep and make them bleed
If the farmer sees it he will shoot it
Because trespassers will be persecuted.

Underneath the poem was another picture, of a man with a smoking gun, a white sheep with red blobs all over it, and a very dead-looking dog lying on its back with its legs in the air.

"It's a very good poem, Sophie," her teacher had said.

"It is, isn't it," Sophie said.

"And it rhymes beautifully."

"It does, doesn't it."

"But could you shoot someone's dog like that, when you're a farmer, I mean?"

"A lady farmer," Sophie said. "No, I couldn't."

"Why not?"

"Lady farmers don't have guns."

"But suppose you did?"

"I still shan't shoot any dogs."

"Because you couldn't do such a thing, you mean?"

"No, because I shan't keep any sheep."

"I never seem to be able to get the better of Sophie," said her teacher to the head-mistress.

"You don't surprise me. How's your farming project coming along?"

"Quite well, I think. If I go wrong, there's always Sophie to put me right. Or Andrew."

"Let's see, it's tomorrow that you're taking your class on a visit to a farm, isn't it?"

"Yes."

"Good luck."

Before the coach arrived, Sophie's teacher checked to see that every child was wearing wellies (because it would be mucky on the farm) and an anorak (because it looked like rain). She made sure that everyone had brought a lunch-box, and told them all that they were not to open them on the coach.

"You've only just had your breakfasts," she said, "so you can wait till midday."

On the coach the children sat in pairs, either side of the central gangway. Andrew sat with Sophie, because she had told him to. Opposite them, short fat Duncan plumped himself down beside tall thin Dawn. Dawn's parents spoiled her, always buying her lots of sweets, and Duncan, who was very greedy, knew that she would have a pocketful. Because he doubted that the contents of his lunch-box would be enough for him, he had secreted in his own anorak pocket a full packet of chocolate biscuits.

On the drive through the countryside the children gazed out of the windows of the coach with cries of, "Oh look, cows!" or, "There's a tractor!" For Sophie, the lady farmer, and Andrew, the farmer's son, this was not good enough, and they set the record straight by adding, "They're Friesians" or, "It's a John Deere."

Only Duncan was not interested in the passing scene. In between wheedling sweets from Dawn he was quietly stuffing himself with chocolate biscuits. The teacher, sitting right at the rear of the coach with a couple of mothers who had come along to help, did not notice. Sophie did.

She nudged Andrew and pointed across.

"I should think he'll make himself sick," she said.

Andrew nodded.

After a while the combination of the swaying coach and the sweets and biscuits began to take effect upon Duncan. He turned pale and shifted uncomfortably in his seat.

"He's going to be sick soon," said Sophie.

Andrew nodded.

Then there was a groan from Duncan and a squeal from Dawn.

"Yuk!" said Sophie. "He's been sick."

"And how!" said Andrew.

"What's all the fuss about?" called the teacher.

"Duncan's been sick on Dawn," said Sophie.

The teacher, experienced in coach trips, had brought with her a bucket, a cloth and a roll of kitchen paper. Armed with these, she came hurrying down the gangway.

"It's OK," Sophie said. "He did it over her wellies."

"My new wellies!" wailed Dawn, for they had indeed been shiningly new and of a horrid pink colour.

The teacher looked at Duncan, who was pale green.

"Did you open your lunch-box?" she asked.

Duncan shook his head.

"No," he said truthfully.

After she had mopped up, the teacher found the lunch-box and looked inside it. It was crammed full of food.

"Have you been giving him something, Dawn?" the teacher asked. Dawn shook her head.

"No," she lied.

The teacher turned to Sophie opposite.

"Did you see Duncan eating?" she said.

Sophie did not approve of telling lies.

"Yes," she said.

"Was Dawn feeding him?"

But Sophie also did not approve of telling tales, so she did not answer.

"Was she, Andrew?"

"Yes," said Andrew, "she was giving him

sweets and he was eating chocolate biscuits and they never offered none of them to us, not neither of them. They're greedy, they are."

"It's enough to make you sick," said Sophie.

The farm to which they were going was one that was regularly visited by parties of schoolchildren, and the farmer's wife was waiting, ready to show them round.

The first thing she did was to give each child a little paper bag full of corn, to feed to all the many hens and ducks and geese, not to mention a number of piglets, that were ranging freely about the farmyard. At the sight of the children, these came hurrying up, while from a dovecot at one end of the yard a cloud of white pigeons came fluttering down to join in the feast.

There were "Oohs!" and "Aahs!" of delight from the children as the birds scratched about around their feet and even took grains of wheat from their hands. One or two, Dawn especially, seemed nervous of some of the bigger birds, particularly a white gander that flapped his wings, stretched out his long neck, and hissed at them. Duncan, his appetite restored as well as his colour, chewed some of the corn thoughtfully before deciding he didn't much like the taste.

It did not occur to Sophie to be frightened of the gander. She plodded up and stood before him. Putting her hands on her hips, she flapped her elbows, stretched out her short neck, and hissed back at him. Embarrassed, the gander let out a loud honk and hastily led his wives away.

The farmer's wife, standing near, said to

66

Sophie's teacher, "Well, she's certainly not frightened of animals."

Sophie remembered something that Aunt Al had said to her long ago, when she had been a bit wary of earwigs, and she used the same words now.

"No good being scared of animals if you're going to be a farmer," she said.

"Oh, you are, are you?" said the farmer's wife. "It's hard work, you know."

"I don't mind," Sophie said.

"And you have to get up very early."

"I like that."

"And you have to be out in all winds and weathers."

"That doesn't worry me."

"It's messy too – mucking out all the animals."

"I like doing that," said Sophie. "I clean out my rabbit Beano every day and put it all on a special rabbit dung heap that I make. It's good for the garden, it helps its futility."

"Fertility," said Sophie's teacher behind her hand.

"Anyway," said Sophie, "I think manure smells lovely. Cow is nice, and so is pig, but horse is best of all."

"Well, you'll be all right then," said the farmer's wife, "because we've got cows and pigs and horses to show you and a lot of other animals too. You'll get all the smells you could want."

Sophie had a lovely morning. As well as ordinary breeds of farm animals, there were some rare ones too, and Sophie thought how nice these would look on her farm when she should get it.

As well as Blossom and April and May

and Shorty and Measles, she felt she really must have a Longhorn cow because its horns were so long (and a Dexter cow because its legs were so short), and some Polish hens with feather hats on their heads, and a tiny miniature horse called a Falabella, and a Middle White pig with a squashed-in face.

"I'll just have to have a bigger farm," she said to Andrew.

At midday they ate their packed lunches in a huge old barn. All were hungry by now and they ate greedily, none more greedily than Duncan, who, despite being half the size of some of the other children, seemed to have brought twice as much food.

After lunch the farmer himself appeared, leading a great big black Shire horse with huge hairy legs and feet like soup-plates, whose name was Henry VIII. Behind Henry

VIII, trundling along over the cobblestones of the yard, was the most enormous four-wheeled wagon, painted red, white and blue, and called, so the farmer told them, the Ark Royal.

And everyone climbed aboard the Ark Royal, two by two, and off they all went for a tour of the farm. Sophie sat right at the front of the wagon, just behind Henry VIII's enormous bottom, and thought how beautiful and how strong he was, and how she simply must have one like him for her farm.

Only when they were almost back in the farmyard did it begin to rain, but then it tipped down, and everyone got off the Ark Royal and hurried down the yard towards the coach, which was by now waiting for them at the farm gate.

Safely inside, the teacher walked along the gangway, counting to make sure everyone was aboard.

She came to the place where Dawn and Duncan were seated on one side. On the other was Andrew, alone.

"Where's Sophie?" she asked him.

Andrew jerked a thumb towards the window.

"Saying goodbye to Henry VIII," he said.

Looking out, the teacher could see the short stocky figure of Sophie, standing in the pouring rain, stroking the lowered velvety muzzle of the great black horse. She went to the door of the coach and called, "Sophie! Hurry up!"

"Please, miss," cried Dawn, "I don't want to sit by Duncan. He might do it again."

"Oh, go and sit by Andrew, Duncan," said the teacher, and again she called, "Come on, Sophie! Quickly!"

If Sophie hadn't been hurrying, if the yard hadn't been generously covered with the droppings of chickens and ducks and geese and piglets, and if the rain hadn't turned all that into a stinking slimy soup, it might not have happened.

As it was, Sophie slipped and fell with a splash.

"Are you all right, Sophie?" asked the teacher anxiously when at last the lady farmer arrived at the coach.

"Bit dirty," said Sophie cheerfully, holding out hands that were plastered with muck. Her clothes were covered in it, her face splashed with it.

"And a bit pongy," she added.

"Phew!" cried the other children as Sophie passed by on her way to her seat. But it was filled.

"Sit next to Dawn, Sophie," the teacher called.

Sophie looked at Dawn's horrified face and grinned.

"Don't mind if I do," she said.

Sophie was a rat.

SOPHIE AT THE CONCERT

Sophie had a calendar on her bedroom wall.

It bore a picture of an old-fashioned farming scene – thatched buildings, round haystacks, a duckpond and, between the shafts of a cart, a horse something like Henry VIII, led by a small boy in a smock-frock.

Under the picture was written:

To plough and sow,
To reap and mow,
And to be a farmer's boy.

Sophie had crossed out the last two words

and written "lady farmer" instead. She also crossed out each day that passed as she waited anxiously for two very important dates, round each of which she had drawn a big red circle.

The first was of course Christmas Day – her birthday – and the second was New Year's Day, when she would start her riding lessons at Cloverlea Stables.

In the meantime the class's farming topic was finished, and everyone was preparing for the school's Christmas concert.

Last year Matthew and Mark had been Tweedledum and Tweedledee in a production of bits of *Alice* (both *in Wonderland* and *Through the Looking-glass*). Sophie had been what she called "a crowd" in what she called an "activity play".

Unfortunately her father had told her what crowd players are supposed to say, so that while everyone in the Nativity play was quite silent when the Wise Men presented their gifts to the infant Jesus, Sophie shouted, "Rhubarb, rhubarb, rhubarb!"

This year the juniors were doing *The Wizard of Oz*, and the twins were Munchkins.

The infants were to do a play based on the story of *The Pied Piper of Hamelin*. There were plenty of parts in this for everyone – the Piper himself, the Mayor and Corporation, the townspeople, their children, and of course the rats.

Sophie was a rat.

She did not say anything to her parents (because she did not approve of whingeing) but she was secretly disappointed not to have been given a bigger part. Being a rat was no better than being a crowd, worse, in fact, for all the rats were allowed to do was squeak.

What she would really have liked to have been was the Piper, dressed in a wonderful red and yellow costume and playing "Come, follow, follow, follow" at the head of, first, all the rats, and, later, all the children.

Truth to tell, Sophie's teacher had considered her for the part, simply because Sophie was quite good at playing the recorder. But the Piper, the teacher knew, was meant to be male and tall and thin, none of which applied to Sophie, so she gave the part to a tall, thin recorder-playing boy called Justin.

But then, only two days before the concert, Fate took a hand as Justin took a tumble out of a tree and broke his arm. It was not a bad break, but all the same it isn't possible to play a recorder with one arm in plaster.

Hastily, Sophie's teacher held an audition

of several other recorder players, including Sophie. Not only did Sophie play "Come, follow, follow, follow" just as well as Justin had, but it turned out that she, unlike the others, had learned the Piper's words as well.

"And she shouts them out good and loud," her teacher told the headmistress. "Sophie may not be the world's best actor, but when she says, 'I will rid your town of rats,' you believe her. And when she stumps up to the Mayor and demands her thousand guilders for doing the job, you wonder how he dare refuse her."

At home, after the audition, Sophie said to the family, "You know our play."

"Yes," her mother said.

"*The Pied Piper of Hamelin*, isn't it?" her father said.

"Sophie's a rat!" sniggered the Munchkins.

Sophie resisted the temptation to call her brothers mowldy, stupid and assive.

Instead she said with dignity, "Actually, I am not a rat any more."

"Have you got the sack?" asked Mark.

"Did you forget your squeaks?" asked Matthew.

"No," said Sophie. "It's just that they needed an understeady."

"Understudy," said her mother. "For what?"

"Well, Justin's bust his arm so he can't do it, so they held an addition."

"Audition," said her father.

"For the Pied Piper, d'you mean?" asked Matthew.

"Yes," said Sophie.

"Who's going to do it then?" asked Mark.

"Me," said Sophie. "I am the Pied Piper of Hamelin."

They all stared at Sophie, short and stocky, her dark hair looking, as always, as though she had just come through a hedge backwards, and all of them knew that, though small, she was very determined.

"If anyone can make a good job of it," her father said, "you will."

"I'm so pleased for you, darling," her mother said, and even the twins said, with one voice, "Good luck, Sophie."

"Thanks," said Sophie. "It'll be all right on the night."

And indeed it was.

The Wizard of Oz went very well, even though two of the Munchkins seemed rather more active and noisy than the rest.

But *The Pied Piper of Hamelin,* everyone agreed afterwards, was something else.

From the moment Sophie plodded on to the stage, in "queer long coat" (made for

Sophie played the tune of "Come, follow, follow, follow" as loudly as she could.

Justin, so much *too* long) "half of yellow and half of red" and began to play, there was no doubt that all *would* follow the small determined Piper for the rest of their lives.

Down off the stage, and among the audience, and all around the school hall plodded the Pied Piper, while behind her, first the rats scuttled and squeaked, and later, the children of Hamelin skipped and danced. And all the time Sophie played the tune of "Come, follow, follow, follow" as loudly as she could, over and over and over again. What's more, she hardly made any mistakes, except once when she tripped over the skirts of that long coat, and then towards the end, when she ran out of puff.

How the audience cheered when it was over!

First, the Mayor (Andrew – a large cushion strapped to his tummy underneath his robes) came forward to the front of the stage and bowed, and then his Corporation, and then the townsfolk, and then their children (including one tall girl with fair hair done in bunches and tied with green ribbons), and then the rats (including one small fat boy rat who looked greedy enough to eat a whole cheese on his own).

But the loudest applause was reserved for the last to come forward, the Piper.

"Take your hat off and bow, Sophie," her teacher whispered, as she pushed her out from the wings. And Sophie swept off her pointed cap, half red, half yellow, and bowed so low she nearly overbalanced.

That night Sophie went to bed very happy.

"I'm proud of you, Sophie," her teacher had said.

"Well done indeed, Sophie," the headmistress had said.

And when they got home, her mother and father had told her that she'd been the star of the show, and the ex-Munchkins had actually called her brilliant.

Sophie fell asleep still grinning.

When she woke next morning, she crossed off the previous day's date on the calendar. There were only a few left now until it would be Christmas and her birthday.

She got back into bed and addressed Tomboy, who was lying on her duvet as usual.

"Do you know, my dear," she said, "that I am going to be seven?"

"*Yeee-ooo?*" said the black cat in amazement, it seemed to Sophie.

"Yes, I am, and about time too. I've been six for years and years."

"*Neeee-o,*" said Tomboy.

"Well, one year anyway, but it seems like ages."

Sophie tickled the base of Tomboy's ears, making her purr like mad. Looking at her cat's sleek black coat made her think of Tomboy's son Ollie, who was also coal black, and thinking of Ollie made her think of Aunt Al, to whom Ollie belonged.

"Wouldn't it be nice," she said, "if only Aunt Al could be here to see me when I start my riding lessons? She's paying for them, after all. It's a pity she's so far away, stuck up on top of those old Highlands. I dare say she's sometimes lonely, with only a black cat for company."

"Meee-ow?" said Tomboy.

"No, not you, my dear. Your son Ollie," said Sophie.

She sighed.

"I wish Aunt Al could come to stay," she

said, "but no such luck, I'm afraid."

Then she began to rub the tip of her nose.

"Tomboy," she said, "in case you didn't know, black cats are supposed to be lucky. But only if they come to you from the right-hand side. Let's see what you can do," and she lifted her cat up and dropped her off the bed, on the right-hand side of it.

Tomboy stretched herself, hooping her back and scrabbling at the carpet, and then jumped straight back up. For extra luck, Sophie crossed her fingers, on both hands.

"I wish Aunt Al could come to stay," she said again.

At breakfast, Sophie was eating Coco Pops, while Puddle sat hopefully at her feet, waiting for her to drop some.

Matthew and Mark had gobbled their food at top speed as usual and disappeared.

Sophie's father was reading a newspaper.

Her mother was opening a letter.

She read it, and then said to her husband quietly, "It's from You-know-who."

"Oh," said Sophie's father from behind his paper. "Can she come?"

"Yes."

"For Christmas?"

"No. For Hogmanay, she says, and for a week after that."

Sophie swallowed a mouthful of Coco Pops.

"What's Hogmanay?" she asked.

"It's a special day for people in Scotland, the last day of the year."

I only know one person in Scotland, Sophie thought. She suddenly paused in the act of putting a loaded spoonful in her mouth. The spoon tilted a little and Puddle cleared up.

"Who's You-know-who?" she said.

Her father lowered his paper and looked at his wife and they smiled.

"Guess," they said.

"Aunt Al?" said Sophie softly.

"Yes."

"Coming to stay with us?"

"Yes. She arrives on the thirty-first of December."

"Yikes!" cried Sophie. "Tomboy did the trick!"

*"Why don't you say something nice to her,
Sophie?" said Aunt Al.*

SOPHIE IN THE DOG-HOUSE

Christmas Day came and went. For Sophie it had the usual bonus – two presents from each person, one with "Happy Christmas" on it, one with "Many Happy Returns".

But Sophie had made sure that the other members of the family were not forgotten. She had raided her Farm Money and had bought what she thought were suitable gifts.

For her father – a large box of matches, to help him light that pipe of his that seemed always to be going out.

For her mother – a large bar of Lifebuoy soap. ("Not that you aren't quite clean,

Mum," she said, "but this smells different from our usual stuff.")

For Matthew and Mark – sweets, as usual.

For Tomboy – a piece of coley from the fishmonger. ("Its real name is coalfish," he had told her. "Good," said Sophie. "Just right for a coal black cat.")

For Puddle – a big bone from the butcher.

For Beano – the biggest carrot in the greengrocer's.

For only one person had Sophie not bought anything, and that was the person who was going to give her the biggest, most expensive present ever, the course of riding lessons.

How could she compete with that? Whatever should she get Aunt Al? After Christmas she consulted her mother, who thought for a while and then said, "You know, rather than buying her something,

I think that what Aunt Al would like best would be if you made her something, did it all by yourself, just for her, a special present."

"I can't make things," Sophie said. "I'm no good at that."

"I know!" her mother said. "Write her a poem. You did a lovely poem for your farming topic – your teacher showed me. Do one for Aunt Al."

"What about?"

"Well, it could be part of a Christmas card. You could draw a picture and write a poem too."

"But Christmas is over."

"Well, a New Year card then."

"OK," Sophie said. "I'll have a bash."

She did the picture first. After a lot of thought, she decided to draw a black cat. Cats weren't as hard to do as some things, and it was easy to colour it in with a black felt marker. Of course she drew it walking from right to left. Then she wrote OLLIE under it. The poem took longer, but Sophie worked away determinedly at it, occasionally asking questions like, "What rhymes with 'Scotland'?" or "What rhymes with 'the Highlands'?" or, "How old's Aunt Al going to be next year?"

At last she finished it, the day before Aunt Al was due to arrive. To Sophie's surprise, her father set off quite early on the morning of December the thirty-first to fetch his great-aunt from the railway station.

"The train's due in at nine a.m.," he said.

"Yikes!" cried Sophie. "You said she lived six hundred miles away. If she only started out this morning, it must be the fastest train in the world."

"No, no," her father said. "It's a ten-hour

journey, but she has a sleeping compart-
ment, you see. She'll have slept nearly all the
way, I hope."

And indeed when Aunt Al did arrive, she
looked as fresh as a daisy. Sophie waited
till everyone else had gone off to do something or other, and then she produced her
special present.

"I did this for you," she said. "It took an
awful long time."

Aunt Al took the card in her skinny, bony
old hands, curled like a bird's claws, and
looked at the picture of the black cat, and
read beneath it:

This is a poem for you Aunt Al
Because you are my speshial pal
And this year Mummy told me
You are going to be 83
So I wish you a Happy New Year

And I hope you will have a nice stay here
Where it is warmer than Scotland
Which is not a hot land
Speshially on top of the Highlands
The coldest place in the British Ilands
And the picture is of Ollie
And you can see his sister Dolly
Because she lives at Cloverlea
Riding Stables where I shall be
Going to ride on Saturday
And you are going to pay
So I am very pleased.
With love from your great great neece.

"It's a very good poem, Sophie," Aunt Al said.

"It is, isn't it," Sophie said.

"And it rhymes beautifully."

"It does, doesn't it."

"And it's the very nicest present you could

have given me," said Aunt Al. "I shall treasure it. And talking of treasuring things, I brought something to show you."

She rummaged in her handbag and brought out an old snapshot.

"Have a look at that," she said.

Sophie took the photograph and studied it. It was not very clear and the picture was rather brownish, but she could see that it was of a small girl sitting on a pony.

"Who d'you think that is?" Aunt Al asked.

"Don't know," said Sophie. "Nobody I know."

"Turn it over then," said Aunt Al, so Sophie did, and written on the back in rather spidery and faded grown-up's writing was:

Alice on Frisk
Balnacraig 1920

"It's you!" Sophie said.

"Yes. I was nine."

"And was Frisk your pony?"

"Yes. He was rather a naughty pony but I loved him more than anything in the world."

"More than your mum and dad?"

"Well, no, perhaps not. But next best after them."

"I wish I could have a pony of my own," said Sophie.

"Wait till you're a lady farmer," said Aunt Al, "and then have a horse, that's my advice. Now tell me – your first lesson is tomorrow, is that right?"

"Yes. It's not really the first. I did some riding in Cornwall."

"How much do you know about the tack?"

"Well," said Sophie, "there's a bridle and reins and a saddle. Oh, and a thing round the pony's tummy."

"The girth. What about a snaffle, what's that?"

"Don't know."

"It's a kind of bit, that goes in the horse's mouth, but it's jointed, so it isn't as harsh as a curb. And what's a numnah?"

"Don't know."

"It's a cloth or pad, a sheepskin sometimes, that goes under the saddle to stop it chafing."

"Gosh, you know a lot, Aunt Al," Sophie said.

"I was a good horsewoman once. Shall I tell you what I think will happen tomorrow?"

"Yes, please."

"Well, you'll all be riding your ponies inside an enclosed ring called a menage, and all round this ring there will be posts at intervals, each with a big letter on it. A K E H C M B F."

99

"Why?"

"So that the instructor can say to you, 'Right, now ride across from A to M,' or E to B, or whatever."

"Oh," said Sophie. "Do they always have those letters?"

"Yes," said Aunt Al, "and they always teach you the same way to remember them. 'All King Edward's Horses Can Manage Big Feeds.'"

"Oh," said Sophie. "I thought King Edward was a potato."

"Oh, Sophie," said Aunt Al. "You're going to be a farmer and no mistake."

Sophie woke on the Saturday morning and looked at the red circle round January the first.

"Happy New Year, my dear," she said to Tomboy, but the black cat only yawned.

Sophie looked at her watch. Seven o'clock. Only three hours to wait now. She got dressed and went downstairs to let Puddle out into the garden and to go to the potting-shed to feed Beano. Again she wished both animals a Happy New Year, but Puddle only barked at her because he wanted her to throw a stick, and Beano only wiffled his nose at her because he never said anything anyway.

At breakfast, though, everyone else returned her good wishes.

"This year," said Sophie's mother to Aunt Al, "Sophie will become a junior."

"Fancy!" said Aunt Al. "Do you look forward to that, Sophie?"

"Yes," said Sophie. "Then I can do judo and throw Dawn down on the mat."

"Who's Dawn?" asked Aunt Al.

"A girl in Sophie's class," said Mark.

"Sophie can't stand her," said Matthew.

"Why not?"

"She's a wimp," said Sophie.

She looked at her watch.

"Only an hour and a half to go," she said. "We ought to be getting ready."

"It's only a ten-minute drive to Cloverlea Stables," her mother said. "By the way, who's coming to watch Sophie's riding lesson?"

"I'm playing golf," said Sophie's father.

"We're playing football," said the twins.

"Aunt Al?"

"Wouldn't miss it for the world. Has she got a hard hat?"

"No," said Sophie's mother. "They supply them with a proper jockey skull cap with a silk over it."

"What about jodhpurs?"

"Jeans will have to do. I dare say some of

the others will have fancy clothes but Sophie doesn't mind, do you, darling?"

"No," said Sophie. "All you need is a good seat."

"Attagirl!" said Aunt Al.

It was a good job that Sophie wasn't fussy, because when they arrived the three other little girls already there were rather smartly dressed. Meg Morris greeted them, and everyone was introduced, including Dolly, who came running up to rub against Sophie.

"We're just waiting for the last of the group," said Meg, and then, "Oh, here she comes now," as another car drew up.

Out of it stepped first Dawn's mother and then Dawn.

"Yuk!" said Sophie loudly.

Dawn was kitted out in skin-tight breeches, polished riding boots, a natty checked hacking jacket, and under it a silk blouse topped by a stock with a gold pin through it. She was even wearing a little bowler hat. She looked a perfect fashion plate. She also looked nervous, until she caught sight of Sophie, when she looked *very* nervous.

Dawn's mother also looked uncomfortable when she recognized Sophie's mother, and they nodded awkwardly at one another as Meg Morris took the five little girls away to introduce them to their ponies.

"Aunt Al," said Sophie's mother. "D'you mind if I just nip off to do some shopping? I shan't be long. I'll be back to see Sophie performing. Will you be all right?"

"Of course," said Aunt Al.

She watched as the five children returned, each leading her pony, and as Meg showed them in turn how to tighten their girths, pull down their stirrups, and then how to mount.

Four of them seemed quite at home in the saddle, but gawky Dawn sat awkwardly, shooting anxious glances towards her mother.

"Now then," said Meg Morris, "I'm going to walk right round with each of you in turn. We'll go on the left rein – that's anti-clockwise – from this post marked A, right round to the post marked F."

"All King Edward's Horses Can Manage Big Feeds," said Sophie.

"Well done, Sophie!" said Meg. "Fancy knowing that!"

Sophie looked pleased.

Three of the other girls looked puzzled.

Dawn looked pale.

As Meg Morris moved off around the menage with the first of the children, Aunt Al came forward to the rails to stand beside

Sophie's pony.

"Sophie," she said in a low voice. "That girl behind you. D'you know her?"

"Not half," said Sophie. "That's Dawn, that is."

"She's nervous," said Aunt Al.

"Of course she is," said Sophie. "She's a wimp," and she looked round scornfully at Dawn.

"We can't all be brave, you know," said Aunt Al. "Why don't you say something nice to her, to encourage her?"

"You must be joking," said Sophie rudely.

"I am not joking, Sophie," said Aunt Al, and there was a steely edge to her voice. "If you cannot do a simple kindness, then though this is your first lesson, it may well be your last. I am not paying out good money for bad behaviour," and she turned away and walked off on her thin bird's legs.

Sophie went very red in the face.

Then she turned in her saddle to face Dawn, who looked, if possible, even more unhappy at this.

"What's the matter with you?" said Sophie gruffly.

"I don't like it," said Dawn miserably. "I might fall off."

Sophie looked at Dawn's long legs.

"Well, it isn't far if you do," she said.

"I'm frightened," said Dawn.

Sophie took a deep breath.

"Look, Dawn," she said in as kindly a voice as she could manage, "you'll be all right. There's nothing to be scared of. All you've got to do is sit there and the lady will hold on to your bridle. You can't come to any harm, honestly. And if you don't like it, well, then you needn't come back here any more."

And I hope you don't, she thought.

So amazed was Dawn to be spoken to by Sophie in such an almost friendly way that she quite forgot her fears and allowed herself to be led around in a daze.

Her mother watched, smiling.

Aunt Al watched, poker-faced.

Sophie's mother returned from her shopping in time to see her daughter being told to "Walk on".

It did not take Meg Morris long to realize that Sophie, for all her lack of experience, was a natural rider, and she treated her differently from the others, who watched admiringly, especially the now pink-cheeked Dawn. Soon she had Sophie changing rein, to go clockwise around the menage, and then it was "Trot on", with Sophie rising in her saddle to the manner born.

When the lesson was over, and Sophie

plodded up to join them, her mother said, "Well done, darling, you rode very well."

Aunt Al said, "Well done, Sophie. Now you can look forward to the rest of your riding lessons."

She looked directly down at Sophie with her sharp blue eyes, and Sophie knew exactly what she meant, and they grinned at one another.

"She does ride well, doesn't she?" said Sophie's mother.

"Not bad," said Aunt Al. "Just needs a touch of the whip now and then."

Sophie found herself flinging her arms round Aunt Al's skinny middle and burying her face against her.

Sophie at the Farm

Aunt Al's visit ended before Sophie's second riding lesson. They parted the best of friends.

"I shall have your poem framed and hang it on my bedroom wall, Sophie," Aunt Al said. "And mind and let me know how the rest of the lessons go. I think you'll make a fine horsewoman."

"Horsegirl," Sophie said.

"Yes, but time flies, and you'll be a woman before you can say 'Jack Robinson'."

"Jack Robinson!" said Sophie quickly, grinning.

"And when you're a bit older, you must

come and visit me and Ollie. You'd love the Highlands."

"Just me, alone?" said Sophie.

"Well, it would be nice if all the family could come, this summer perhaps – your father talks about having a Scottish holiday one year – but yes, I should like it very much if you came by yourself, once you're old enough to make the journey on your own. Say in about – let's see – eight years' time, when you'll be fifteen."

Sophie did a sum in her head.

"But you'll be ninety then," she said, "if..." and she stopped.

"If I haven't kicked the bucket, you were going to say," said Aunt Al. "Don't worry, Sophie, I have every intention of scoring a century and getting that telegram from the Queen. My father lived to be a hundred and two and three-quarters, so I've got form."

"Will Ollie still be alive?" Sophie asked.

"Don't see why not. He's still got all nine lives left."

When it came to the actual time to say goodbye, Sophie supposed they would shake hands, as they always had done before. Neither of them were great kissers. But as it was, she found herself flinging her arms round Aunt Al's skinny middle and burying her face against her, while her great-great-aunt stroked her tousled mop of dark hair. And as Aunt Al was driven away to the railway station while they all waved goodbye, Sophie shouted, "See you!" and Aunt Al called back, "Sure thing!" and then she was gone.

The following day Sophie went to Cloverlea Stables for her second lesson. To her relief, she found that Dawn had not turned up. She had not wanted to go on being nice to her, and now she needn't.

"Is Dawn ill?" she said to Meg Morris.

"No," said Meg. "She's not coming any more."

"Oh dear," said Sophie. "What a shame."

"I think perhaps she's not the horsy type," said Meg.

"No," said Sophie. "She wants to be a hairdresser."

She knew this because last term her class had had to write down what they would like to be when they grew up.

A lot of boys wanted to be professional footballers or racing drivers, and nursing or teaching were popular choices for the girls, though there were several, including Dawn, who chose hairdressing. Andrew of course wrote "Farmer" and Sophie "Lady Farmer".

Duncan wrote "Cook", and when asked why, said simply, "I like food".

At the start of the new term, Sophie tackled her father on the subject of pocket money. Due to the cost of the Christmas presents she had bought, her Farm Money was now down to nine pounds, ten pence.

"I've been collecting for three years," she said to her father, "so I'm only making about three pounds a year. What d'you call someone who is really poor?"

"A pauper?" said her father.

"Well," said Sophie, "I'm pauper than anyone else."

She had worked out a sum on a piece of paper and now she produced it.

"Look," she said. "I want to have enough money to buy a farm by the time I'm grown up, which is eighteen these days, which is in eleven years and three times eleven is thirty-three, plus what I've got now makes forty-two pounds, ten. How am I going to become a lady farmer if I've only got forty-two pounds?"

"Perhaps you'll marry a farmer," her father said. "That's one way to do it."

"I am not marrying Andrew unless he gets his father's farm," said Sophie.

"When the father retires, you mean?"

"Or dies," said Sophie matter-of-factly. "He's quite old."

I shouldn't think he's forty yet, thought Sophie's father. About my age in fact.

"Well, you'll just have to save harder, Sophie," he said.

"I ought to be on Family Insistence," Sophie said.

"Assistance, you mean?"

"You can call it what you like," said

Sophie. "I mean, more pocket money. I'm seven now. I ought to have one pound a week, like Matthew and Mark do. It's not fair. I get 50p and they get two pounds."

"But there are two of them."

"It's all because I'm a girl," said Sophie. "Women ought to be paid the same as men."

Sophie's father felt himself wilting before his daughter's determination.

"Oh, very well then," he said. "I'll put your pocket money up to one pound a week."

"Thanks, Daddy," said Sophie.

She consulted her piece of paper again.

"It's more than two weeks since my birthday," she said, "so now you owe me two extra 50ps already."

"Oh, Sophie," said her father. "You're going to be a businesswoman and no mistake. Andrew could do worse. He'll be a lucky chap if he decides to marry you."

Sophie rubbed the tip of her nose.

"He won't decide," she said, "but you've given me an idea."

In the playground next day Sophie said to Andrew, "I haven't been to tea with you yet this term."

"It's only the second day," said Andrew.

"I still haven't been. You'd better get your mum to ask me."

"Oh, all right."

So a couple of days after that, Andrew's mother asked Sophie's mother if Sophie could come to tea.

"I'll try to keep her from falling in cowpats or into the duckpond," she said.

Before tea Andrew's father took both children to have a look at a sow that had had a litter of ten piglets only the night before. As they looked through the bars of the pen in which the sow lay nursing her already fat pink babies, Sophie said to Andrew's father, "How old are you?"

"I'll be forty this year," he said.

"When are you going to retire?"

Andrew's father smiled.

"Not yet awhile, Sophie," he said. "In another twenty years perhaps, when Andrew's old enough to take over."

"Oh," said Sophie. "He's going to, is he?"

"I hope so. This farm's been handed down from father to son for a long time now."

"I shall drive all the tractors," Andrew said.

"He's clever with his hands," said his father. "Makes some wonderful models with Lego. Should be good with the mechanical side of things."

"I'm going to be a lady farmer, you know,"
said Sophie.

"I'm good with animals," said Sophie. "I'm going to be a lady farmer, you know."

Andrew's father looked at the two seven-year-olds, one very fair, almost white-haired, one dark, standing side by side at the pig pen. Just suppose … in twenty years' time … he said to himself. Andrew could do worse.

After tea Andrew and Sophie were watching children's TV. At least, Andrew was watching. Sophie was thinking. Presently she said, "How much pocket money do you get?"

"One pound a week," said Andrew.

Sophie nodded. I was right, she thought.

"And how much money have you got saved?" she said.

"About two hundred pounds," said Andrew.

"Don't be silly, Andrew," said Sophie.

"How much really?"

"I got twenty pounds altogether for Christmas that I haven't spent yet."

"You don't want to go spending it," Sophie said. "You want to save it."

"Oh, all right," said Andrew, who wanted to watch the programme uninterrupted.

"You ought to be able to save 50p a week," said Sophie.

"Oh, all right."

"And if I can do the same, well, in twenty years' time we'll have a nice lot between us. And then I shan't have to buy a farm and the animals will all be here already and your dad can have a nice rest and you'll be the farmer and I'll be the lady farmer."

Andrew, glued to the screen, did not answer.

Sophie sighed.

"Andrew," she said, "listen to me."

"What?"

"When we're grown up, I'm going to marry you."

"Oh, all right."

That evening, when Sophie's parents came to her bedroom to say good night, she was looking, they thought, particularly happy. Tomboy, lying on her feet, was purring loudly.

"What's up with you?" her mother said. "You look like the cat that's eaten the cream."

"They look like two cats," her father said, "that have eaten two lots of cream."

"Well," said Sophie, "I've something to tell you. I'll write to Aunt Al and tell her, but don't say anything to the boys, they wouldn't understand."

"Understand what?" they said. "What is it you've got to tell us?"

Sophie sat up in bed.

"I wanted you to be the first to know," she said. "I'm engaged."

THE SOPHIE STORIES
by Dick King-Smith
illustrated by David Parkins

Sophie's Snail
Sophie's Tom
Sophie Hits Six
Sophie in the Saddle
Sophie's Lucky

If you enjoyed this book, then you'll be pleased to know that there are five more great stories in paperback about Sophie – featuring a large supporting cast of creatures of all shapes and sizes!

"Rich in humour with a tremendous understanding of what makes small children tick."
Susan Hill, The Sunday Times

"Humorous and touching... Parkins' intense cross-hatched line drawings are classics."
The Guardian

MORE WALKER PAPERBACKS
For You to Enjoy

☐ 0-7445-7725-X   *Sophie's Snail*
                   by Dick King-Smith   £3.99

☐ 0-7445-7726-8   *Sophie's Tom*
                   by Dick King-Smith   £3.99

☐ 0-7445-7721-7   *Sophie Hits Six*
                   by Dick King-Smith   £3.99

☐ 0-7445-7722-5   *Sophie in the Saddle*
                   by Dick King-Smith   £3.99

☐ 0-7445-7724-1   *Sophie's Lucky*
                   by Dick King-Smith   £3.99

☐ 0-7445-6931-1   *Here Comes Tod!*
                   by Philippa Pearce   £3.50

☐ 0-7445-7701-2   *Dog Star*
                   by Jenny Nimmo   £3.99

Name _____

Address _____

_____